For Mum and Dad

First published in 2001

This paperback edition first published in Great Britain in 2003 by
Pavilion Children's Books
64 Brewery Road
London N7 9NT
www.chrysalisbooks.co.uk

A member of **Chrysalis** Books plc

Text © Lynn Roberts 2001
Illustrations © David Roberts 2001
Design and layout © Breslich & Foss Ltd.

The moral right of the author and illustrator has been asserted

A CIP catalogue record for this book is available from the British Library.

ISBN 1 84365 013 4

Set in Garamond 3
Printed in Italy by Gunti

2 4 6 8 10 9 7 5 3 1

This book can be ordered direct from the publisher. Please contact
the Marketing Department. But try your bookshop first.

Cinderella

An Art Deco Love Story

Retold by Lynn Roberts
Illustrated by David Roberts

Pavilion Children's Books

I N a time not too long ago and in a land much like our own, there lived a young and beautiful girl. Her name was Greta. She lived alone with her father because her mother had died many years before.

Greta's father was a kind man. He could be quite forgetful and could not see anything at all without his glasses. One day he gathered up his papers and set off for the city to attend an important meeting. "Goodbye, Greta dear, I shall be back in two days," he called. When he finally returned after two *weeks*, he had a big surprise.

When her new stepmother saw Greta's fine clothes and jewels, she said, "My girls should have some of these. You do not need them all." Elvira and Ermintrude fought over every piece and left Greta with only one simple frock.

"Greta, your room is perfect for my girls. You can find another," her stepmother said smugly.

So Greta was forced to sleep in the kitchen. At night she lay by the fire to keep warm. When she wakened she was always covered in dust and cinders. Elvira and Ermintrude started calling her "Cinderella", and soon even her father called her by that name. He thought it was just a friendly endearment.

One day, as she was cleaning the house, Cinderella heard an announcement on the radio. She ran to tell her stepmother and stepsisters the exciting news. "The king is to hold a ball in honour of his son, Prince Roderick," Cinderella explained breathlessly. "All the eligible girls in the land are invited. The prince is going to choose a bride!"

There was great excitement on the day of the ball. Cinderella's stepmother knew that Cinderella's beauty outshone that of her own daughters. To make sure Cinderella had no time to prepare for the ball, she made her run back and forth helping Elvira and Ermintrude.

"Brush my hair, Cinderella!" shouted Ermintrude.

"Bring my grey dress," snarled Elvira. "And do my make-up!"

Alone in the kitchen, Cinderella sighed and wiped away a tear as she watched the sisters and their mother drive away in all their finery.

The ball was already in full swing when Cinderella crept in, anxious in case her stepsisters recognized her.

"This is hopeless," Prince Roderick muttered to himself as he prepared to leave. "There is no one here whom I find interesting." Then his eyes fell on Cinderella. In an instant he fell in love.

The prince took Cinderella's hand and led her to the dance floor. They danced together for the rest of the evening and everyone — even her stepsisters — wondered who the beautiful girl could be. Then the clock began to strike midnight. Cinderella, remembering the kindly woman's warning, raced to the door. As she ran down the palace steps, her beautiful clothes began to turn into rags. In her haste she lost one delicate glass slipper on the stairs, but she managed to slip the other into her pocket.

In the car park Cinderella found her leek, rat, mice and glow-worms where the car and chauffeur had been. Gathering them up, she ran home as fast as she could.

Prince Roderick held Cinderella's dainty glass slipper in his hand. "The girl whose foot fits this slipper shall be my bride!" he vowed. He knew that he could never love another.

The next morning, breakfast was interrupted by another announcement on the radio: the prince planned to visit every girl in the land that very day to find the stranger with whom he had danced.

Cinderella's stepmother did not know that Cinderella had been at the ball, and she did not want to take any chances. She was determined that the prince would not see Cinderella's beauty.

"Go and do the laundry," she ordered, to get Cinderella out of the way.

Meanwhile, Elvira and Ermintrude prepared themselves for the royal visit.

At last the prince arrived. After greeting him, Elvira tried the shoe on, but her foot was too wide. Then Ermintrude pushed her foot into the tiny shoe. For one moment it looked as though it might fit ... but her foot was too long.

"Why not let Cinderella try?" asked her father, coming into the room.

"She was not even at the ball," her stepmother snapped. But the prince saw a familiar pair of eyes peeping out from behind a screen. To the horror of Cinderella's stepmother and stepsisters, Prince Roderick took Cinderella by the hand and led her to the couch. He slipped the shoe on to her foot.

"A perfect fit!" he cried. Cinderella pulled the other shoe from her pocket, and the prince knew that he had found his bride.

Cinderella (for she kept her new name) and her prince were married soon after. Because she had a forgiving nature, Cinderella allowed Ermintrude and Elvira to attend the wedding. And they *almost* managed to behave themselves.

Illustrator's Note

When I was asked to illustrate *Cinderella,* I thought it would be interesting to set the story in the 1930s. I have always had an interest in that period and wanted to incorporate Art Deco designs alongside those of earlier periods. My background in fashion design made it especially fun to research the wardrobe for Cinderella and her wicked stepfamily. In creating these characters, I was influenced by the movie stars, magazine covers, and art of the 1920s and '30s. The paintings that decorate the walls are my humble interpretations of those by Augustus John and Tamara de Lempicka, and the wallpaper, furniture, and pottery are all based on real Art Deco designs.

The illustrations were done in pen and ink with watercolour on hot pressed, heavyweight paper.